Y0-BKB-217

A Robbie Reader

What's So
Great About . . . ?

MARTIN LUTHER
KING JR.

KaaVonia Hinton

Mitchell Lane
PUBLISHERS

P.O. Box 196
Hockessin, Delaware 19707
Visit us on the web: www.mitchelllane.com
Comments? email us: mitchelllane@mitchelllane.com

**Mitchell Lane**
**PUBLISHERS**

Copyright © 2009 by Mitchell Lane Publishers. All rights reserved. No part of this book may be reproduced without written permission from the publisher. Printed and bound in the United States of America.

Printing     1     2     3     4     5     6     7     8     9

### A Robbie Reader/What's So Great About . . . ?

| | | |
|---|---|---|
| Amelia Earhart | Anne Frank | Annie Oakley |
| Christopher Columbus | Daniel Boone | Davy Crockett |
| The Donner Party | Elizabeth Blackwell | Ferdinand Magellan |
| Francis Scott Key | Galileo | George Washington Carver |
| Harriet Tubman | Helen Keller | Henry Hudson |
| Jacques Cartier | Johnny Appleseed | King Tut |
| Lewis and Clark | **Martin Luther King Jr.** | Paul Bunyan |
| Pocahontas | Robert Fulton | Rosa Parks |
| Sam Houston | | |

**Library of Congress Cataloging-in-Publication Data**
Hinton, KaaVonia, 1973–
Martin Luther King, Jr. / by KaaVonia Hinton.
  p. cm. — (A Robbie reader. What's so great about—?)
Includes bibliographical references and index.
ISBN 978-1-58415-724-3 (library bound)
1. King, Martin Luther, Jr., 1929-1968—Juvenile literature. 2. African Americans—Biography—Juvenile literature. 3. Civil rights workers—United States—Biography—Juvenile literature. 4. Baptists—United States—Clergy—Biography—Juvenile literature. 5. African Americans—Civil rights—History—20th century—Juvenile literature. I. Title.
E185.97.K5H55 2009
323.092—dc22
[B]

2008020903

**ABOUT THE AUTHOR:** KaaVonia Hinton is an assistant professor in the Educational Curriculum and Instruction department at Old Dominion University in Norfolk, Virginia. She has written *Angela Johnson: Poetic Prose* (Scarecrow Press) and several books for young readers, including the biography Jacqueline Woodson for Mitchell Lane Publishers.

**PUBLISHER'S NOTE:** The following story has been thoroughly researched and to the best of our knowledge represents a true story. While every possible effort has been made to ensure accuracy, the publisher will not assume liability for damages caused by inaccuracies in the data, and makes no warranty on the accuracy of the information contained herein.

PLB

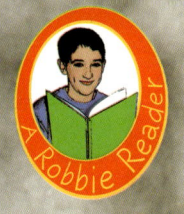

# TABLE OF CONTENTS

**Chapter One**
**Let Freedom Ring** .................................................................. 5

**Chapter Two**
**M.L.** ......................................................................................... 9

**Chapter Three**
**Reverend King** ...................................................................... 13

**Chapter Four**
**Montgomery Bus Boycott** ..................................................... 17

**Chapter Five**
**Celebrate the Dream** ............................................................ 23

**Chronology** ............................................................................ 28
**Timeline in History** ............................................................... 29
**Find Out More** ....................................................................... 30
**Books** .................................................................................... 30
**Works Consulted** .................................................................. 30
**On the Internet** .................................................................... 30
**Glossary** ................................................................................ 31
**Index** ..................................................................................... 32

Words in **bold** type can be found in the glossary.

Martin Luther King Jr. was an organizer and key speaker at the March on Washington for Jobs and Freedom. Other organizers were civil rights leaders A. Philip Randolph and Bayard Rustin.

# CHAPTER ONE

# Let Freedom Ring

On August 28, 1963, more than two hundred thousand people from all over the United States gathered in front of the Lincoln Memorial in Washington, D.C. They were supporting the fight for **civil rights**.

While the group listened to several speakers talk about **discrimination** (dis-krih-mih-NAY-shun), unfair laws, and low-paying jobs, many people were waiting to hear what Dr. Martin Luther King Jr. would say. As president of the Southern **Christian** Leadership Conference (SCLC), a group that supports the struggle for civil rights, King helped organize the March on Washington for Jobs and Freedom.

## CHAPTER ONE

King was a preacher who encouraged people to fight for equal rights. He had worked on his speech all night and was eager to read it. Before he could read everything he had written to the audience, he decided to repeat a phrase he had shared with audiences before: "I have a dream."

He never looked back at his written speech again. Instead, he started to share his hopes and dreams of **equality** (ee-KWAH-lih-tee) with the crowd. "I have a dream that one day . . . in Alabama little black boys and black girls will be able to join hands with little white

In 1954, the Supreme Court ruled that making black children and white children go to separate schools was unfair and against the law. In 1963, when King gave his speech, many black and white children who lived in the northern and southern United States still had to go to separate schools.

## LET FREEDOM RING

King welcomes the thousands of people who came to Washington, D.C., from different parts of the United States of America. He spoke about his dream of a just America to people of all ages, races, and religions. The March on Washington is considered the largest protest event in the United States.

boys and white girls as sisters and brothers," he said.

King's speech during the March on Washington helped the whole world see that the African-American community and its supporters were determined to spread their message: America would not be a great nation until it "let freedom ring" for all of its citizens.

In this house, Martin Luther King Jr. was born. The house, on Auburn Street in Atlanta, Georgia, belonged to his mother's parents, Reverend Adam Daniel Williams and Jennie Celeste Williams. It was built in 1895, and Martin's grandparents bought it in 1909.

## CHAPTER TWO

# M.L.

Martin Luther King Jr. was born on January 15, 1929, in his family's home at 501 Auburn Avenue in Atlanta, Georgia. His father, Martin Luther King Sr., and his mother, Alberta Williams King, were important members of the community. At first his parents named their son Michael Luther King, but his father changed both of their names to Martin in 1935. His friends and family called the boy M.L.

Martin had an older sister named Christine and a younger brother named Alfred Daniel. Their mother encouraged them to be proud of themselves and to work hard to be the very best people they could be. When she explained to them about the cruelty of slavery and the unfairness of **segregation** (seh-greh-GAY-shun)—separating people because of

## CHAPTER TWO

their race—Martin became angry. His mother told him to always remember that no matter what anyone said, he was somebody, he was important. "You are as good as anyone," she said.

M.L. remembered his mother's words. One day his close friend stopped playing with him. When he asked his friend why they could no longer play together, his friend said, "My father said I can no longer play with you because I am white and you are not." This hurt M.L.'s feelings, but his family comforted him.

Another time, M.L. and his father went to a store to buy shoes. They sat down to wait for a white store clerk to help them. Martin and his father became angry when the clerk said, "I'll be happy to wait on you if you'll just move to those seats in the back."

African Americans were sometimes called "colored"—a term that reminds people of the unfair laws that existed in the United States.

The South had laws, sometimes called Jim Crow laws, that required blacks and whites to use "separate but equal facilities." Blacks and whites used separate water fountains, bathrooms, and motels.

Because of Martin and his father's skin color, the clerk would help them only if they moved to the back of the store, where African Americans were served. Martin's father decided that if they were going to be treated poorly because of the color of their skin, he would not buy shoes at that store. M.L. never forgot the unfairness of segregation and discrimination.

Martin Luther King Jr. delivers a sermon at Dexter Avenue Baptist Church in Montgomery, Alabama. King studied religion for three years, then served as an associate (uh-SOH-shee-it) pastor at his father's church for four years before he started preaching at Dexter Avenue.

**CHAPTER THREE**

# Reverend King

M.L. did well in the public schools of Atlanta. After two years in high school, he enrolled in Morehouse College, the college his father had attended. Since M.L. wanted to help people, he planned to become a lawyer or doctor.

By the time he finished school at Morehouse in 1948, his plans had changed. He decided that he wanted to become a **reverend** (REH-vrend) instead. Many of the men in King's family were preachers. The Kings lived down the street from Ebenezer Baptist Church, where M.L.'s father was the pastor and his mother was an organist. After college, King and his brother, Alfred Daniel, became pastors there too.

M.L. took classes in theology (thee-AH-luh-jee), the study of religion, at two schools

13

## CHAPTER THREE

before he met Coretta Scott. She was studying music at the New England Conservatory (kun-SER-vuh-tor-ee) of Music. In 1953, Martin and Coretta were married. They were both from the South and wanted to fight against **unjust** laws there.

Martin and Coretta had four children—two sons (Martin Luther III and Dexter Scott) and two daughters (Yolanda Denise and Bernice Albertine). Martin often played games and read to his children, though he had to spend a large amount of time away from them. While he marched and spoke out against unfair laws, he always thought about how the work he did

Martin Luther King Jr. met Coretta Scott in Boston in 1952. They married the following year at Coretta's parents' home in Marion, Alabama. Martin's father performed the wedding ceremony.

**REVEREND KING**

Martin Luther King Jr. and his wife, Coretta Scott King, are shown with their children (left to right): Dexter Scott, Yolanda Denise, Bernice Albertine (who became a minister like her father), and Martin Luther King III.

would help his children, and children all over the country, to lead better lives someday.

By 1954, Martin and Coretta had moved to Montgomery, Alabama. There, Martin Luther King Jr. would be the pastor of Dexter Avenue Baptist Church.

Rosa Parks was arrested for breaking a bus segregation law. A judge found her guilty during her trial on December 5, 1955. She was fined $10 and had to pay court costs. King (in the background) went to her trial and led the boycott that was sparked by her arrest.

## CHAPTER FOUR

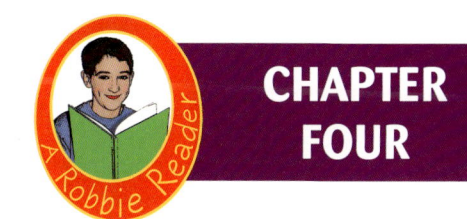

# Montgomery Bus Boycott

Because of segregation, African Americans were forced to ride in the back of the bus, and they had to stand up if white passengers were in need of a seat. On December 1, 1955, Rosa Parks decided to fight against this unfair rule. She did this when she refused to give her seat on a bus to a white man and was arrested.

A few days later, a group was created that would fight against unfair rules such as the one that led to Rosa Parks' arrest. They called themselves the Montgomery Improvement Association, and they named King president of the group. One of the most important things they did, at the suggestion of E.D. Nixon, was organize a **nonviolent** (non-VY-lent) bus **boycott** (BOY-kot).

## CHAPTER FOUR

Edgar Daniel "E.D." Nixon was the president of Montgomery's local chapter of the National Association for the Advancement of Colored People (NAACP). He joined with others to bail Rosa Parks out of jail when she was arrested for refusing to give her seat on a bus to a white man. Later, Nixon was arrested for taking part in the boycott.

King and the other leaders of the Montgomery Improvement Association asked every African American in Montgomery to boycott, or stop riding, the buses until the bus company allowed all riders, despite their race, to sit in any seat they wanted to. The African-American community of Montgomery walked, rode mules and bicycles, carpooled, and took taxis because they did not want to support a bus company that did not treat them with respect and fairness.

Some people did not like it when King encouraged African Americans to fight for equal rights. They called King's home and made threats. His house was bombed and he was

**MONTGOMERY BUS BOYCOTT**

**assaulted**. **Hate crimes** were also directed at his parents. Despite the violence directed at his family, King always remained nonviolent and continued to fight against racism.

It took over 380 days to do it, but finally, on November 13, 1956, the United States Supreme Court said that bus segregation laws were not fair.

Thousands of people banded together to protest segregation in schools, buses, and other public places.

# CHAPTER FOUR

Ralph Abernathy, Martin Luther King Jr., and Bayard Rustin leave the Montgomery County Courthouse in February 1956 after being accused of breaking the city's laws against boycotting. King was found guilty and had to pay a $500 fine.

**MONTGOMERY BUS BOYCOTT**

A month later, King was one of the first to ride the **desegregated** (dee-SEH-greh-gay-ted) buses. A white bus driver smiled and said, "I believe you are Reverend King, aren't you?" When King answered yes, the driver said, "We are glad to have you this morning."

King said thank you and happily took his seat near the front of the bus.

Reverend Ralph Abernathy (left), Reverend Martin Luther King Jr., and Reverend Glenn Smiley (behind unidentified woman) were among the first to ride the buses in Montgomery after the Supreme Court ordered that blacks and whites can sit wherever they choose while riding city buses.

King received the Nobel Peace Prize in 1964. The prize is given to people who have worked hard to make the world a better place to live.

## CHAPTER FIVE

# Celebrate the Dream

In college, King studied the work of Mohandas K. Gandhi, and in 1959 he visited India, where Gandhi used nonviolence to help free his people. Like Gandhi, King wanted his followers to be peaceful and loving, even to people who were mean and unfair. Because of King's teachings, he won the Nobel Peace Prize in 1964. King, who was only thirty-five, was the youngest person to win the award.

King said, "I thought of the Nobel Peace Prize as a prize, a reward, for the . . . fifty thousand Negro people in Montgomery, Alabama, who came to discover that it is better to walk in **dignity** than to ride the buses." He donated the $54,123 he received as prize money to help the fight for civil rights.

**CHAPTER FIVE**

While they were in India, Coretta Scott King (center) and Martin Luther King Jr. (in black suit) met with people who followed the teachings of Mohandas Gandhi. Gandhi (whose portrait is on the wall) inspired King and other civil rights leaders to use nonviolent resistance against unfair rules and prejudice in the United States.

King did more than lead the bus boycott in Montgomery, Alabama. He organized marches and inspired young people to take part in other boycotts and **sit-ins**. His work encouraged people to register to vote, to protest poor housing conditions, and to fight against unfair pay. He also talked to U.S. presidents, including John F. Kennedy and Lyndon B. Johnson. He hoped to encourage them to help make

**CELEBRATE THE DREAM**

everyone in the United States free. King wrote many books and articles that tell about his life, beliefs, and work.

On April 4, 1968, King was planning to march with **sanitation** (saa-nih-TAY-shun) workers to protest low pay and poor working conditions. As he stood on the balcony of the Lorraine Hotel in Memphis, Tennessee, and prepared to make a speech, he was shot and killed.

King (second from right), SCLC aides Hosea Williams and Jesse Jackson, and Ralph Abernathy arrive at the Lorraine Hotel on April 3, 1968. They were organizing a march for sanitation workers, scheduled for the next day.

# CHAPTER FIVE

Coretta Scott King speaks at a demonstration against the Vietnam War in Washington, D.C., in 1970. She and Jesse Jackson (at her elbow) continued to speak out for civil rights after Martin Luther King Jr. died. In 1984 and 1988, Jackson ran for president of the United States.

Shortly after King's death, his wife began working to encourage the country to celebrate King's birthday each year. She also established the Martin Luther King, Jr. Memorial Center in Atlanta, Georgia. Mrs. King wanted the world to remember Martin's courage and hard work.

**CELEBRATE THE DREAM**

Some people celebrate King's birthday by listening to his speeches, visiting the King Memorial Center, doing volunteer work, or participating in marches. By remembering Martin Luther King Jr., we remember to keep working for civil rights for all.

Mrs. King and other people, such as entertainer Stevie Wonder, spent years trying to get the United States to celebrate King's birthday. At last, President Ronald Reagan signed the bill into law, and Martin Luther King Jr. Day became a national holiday. January 20, 1986, was the first day that the United States celebrated this holiday. Since 1986, on the third Monday in January, people all over the country and in over 100 nations around the world remember the contributions Martin Luther King Jr. made to **society**.

# CHRONOLOGY

**1929**    Martin Luther King Jr. is born on January 15 in Georgia.
**1948**    Martin graduates from Morehouse College.
**1951**    He graduates from Crozer Theological Seminary.
**1953**    He marries Coretta Scott. They will have four children (Yolanda Denise, Martin Luther III, Dexter Scott, and Bernice Albertine).
**1955**    Martin graduates from Boston University. Rosa Parks refuses to give up her seat on a bus to a white passenger, and King is chosen to be president of the Montgomery Improvement Association. The Montgomery Bus Boycott begins.
**1956**    The Montgomery Bus Boycott ends and the buses are integrated.
**1957**    The Southern Christian Leadership Conference (SCLC) is created, and Dr. King is named its first president.
**1959**    Martin and Coretta visit India.
**1963**    Dr. King gives his "I Have a Dream" speech at the March on Washington for Jobs and Freedom in Washington, D.C., on August 28.
**1964**    Dr. King receives the Nobel Peace Prize.
**1968**    Martin Luther King Jr. is shot and killed on April 4.
**1974**    His mother is killed while playing the organ at church during services.
**1986**    Martin Luther King Jr. Day is declared a national holiday in the United States.
**2005**    Filmmaker George Lucas donates one million dollars to the Martin Luther King Jr. National Memorial.
**2006**    Coretta Scott King dies on January 30 at the age of 78. Groundbreaking ceremony for the Martin Luther King Jr. National Memorial is held in November.
**2007**    Martin Luther King Jr.'s daughter, Yolanda Denise King, dies on May 15.
**2008**    The W.K. Kellogg Foundation donates three million dollars to the Martin Luther King Jr. National Memorial. A massive radio campaign is held to raise funds for the memorial.

# TIMELINE IN HISTORY

**1863** Lincoln's Emancipation Proclamation ends slavery in the United States.
**1868** The Fourteenth Amendment secures citizenship rights for African Americans.
**1870** The Fifteenth Amendment guarantees voting rights for African Americans.
**1896** The Supreme Court says separate but equal facilities for blacks and whites are legal.
**1906** In India, Mohandas K. Gandhi begins a nonviolent protest against the fighting in his country.
**1913** Rosa Parks is born.
**1920** The Nineteenth Amendment gives women the right to vote.
**1926** Historian Carter G. Woodson starts Black History Week.
**1929** The Great Depression begins in the United States.
**1954** The Supreme Court says schools in the United States should be desegregated.
**1960** Four students at North Carolina Agricultural & Technical State University in Greensboro, North Carolina, try to order food at a Woolworth lunch counter that serves only whites. Their actions spark sit-ins across North Carolina and Virginia.
**1961** The Freedom Riders travel south to protest bus segregation.
**1964** The Mississippi voter registration drive known as Freedom Summer takes place, and the Civil Rights Act is passed.
**1965** Coretta Scott King meets with civil rights leader Malcolm X.
**1967** Thurgood Marshall becomes the first African American Supreme Court Justice.
**1970** Americans celebrate the first Earth Day on April 22.
**1976** Black History Week is extended to Black History Month.
**1984** Civil rights activist and former heavyweight champion Muhammad Ali learns he has Parkinson's disease.
**1986** Civil rights activist John Lewis is elected to Congress.
**1991** Clarence Thomas becomes the second African American Supreme Court Justice.
**1992** Astronaut Mae Jemison is the first African American woman in space.
**1996** The Summer Olympics are held in Atlanta, Georgia.
**2006** Ceremonial groundbreaking takes place on the National Mall for the Dr. Martin Luther King, Jr. Memorial.
**2008** African American Barack Obama wins the Democratic Primary and runs for U.S. president.

# FIND OUT MORE

## Books
Bolden, Tonya. *M.L.K: Journey of a King*. New York: Abrams Books, 2007.
Farris, Christine King. *My Brother Martin: A Sister Remembers Growing Up with the Rev. Dr. Martin Luther King Jr*. New York: Simon & Schuster Books for Young Readers, 2003.
Myers, Walter Dean. *I've Seen the Promised Land: The Life of Dr. Martin Luther King Jr*. New York: HarperCollins, 2004.
Rappaport, Doreen. *Martin's Big Words: The Life of Dr. Martin Luther King Jr*. New York: Jump at the Sun/Hyperion Books for Children, 2001.

## Works Consulted
"A Partner in the Dream." *The Virginian-Pilot*, February 1, 2006.
Bennett, Lerone, Jr. *What Manner of Man: A Biography of Martin Luther King Jr*. Chicago: Johnson, 1964.
Clayborne, Carson, ed. *The Autobiography of Martin Luther King Jr*. New York: Warner Books, 1998.
Frady, Marshall. *Martin Luther King Jr*. New York: Viking, 2002.
Hajela, Deepti. "Time Forgets Scale of His Dream, Some Say." *The Virginian-Pilot*, January 21, 2008.
http://www.redorbit.com/news/general/1223344/time_forgets_scale_of_his_dream_some_say/index.html
Reynolds, Barbara A. "The Real Coretta Scott King." *Washington Post*, February 4, 2006. http://www.washingtonpost.com/wp-dyn/content/article/2006/02/03/AR2006020302512.html

## On the Internet
The King Center: "Martin Luther King, Jr."
http://www.thekingcenter.org
National Park Service: "Martin Luther King, Jr. National Historic Site"
http://www.nps.gov/malu
Nobel Prize: "Martin Luther King, Jr., The Nobel Peace Prize 1964"
http://nobelprize.org/nobel_prizes/peace/laureates/1964/king-bio.html
Time Magazine: "Martin Luther King, Jr."
http://www.time.com/time/time100/leaders/profile/king.html
Washington, D.C. Martin Luther King, Jr. National Memorial
http://www.mlkmemorial.org

PHOTO CREDITS: Cover, pp. 1, 3, 8, 11, 15, 18, 19, 26—Library of Congress; p. 4—Warren K. Leffler; p. 6—JupiterImages; p. 7—U.S. Naval Military Sealift Command; pp. 12, 14—AP Photo; p. 16—National Archives and Records Administration; p. 20—AP Photo/Gene Herrick; p. 21—AP Photo/Harold Valentine; pp. 22, 24, 25—AP Photo; p. 27—Western Washington Fellowship of Reconciliation (WWFOR).

# GLOSSARY

**assaulted** (uh-SOL-ted)—Physically or verbally attacked.

**boycott** (BOY-kot)—To protest by refusing to buy or use products or services.

**Christian** (KRIS-chen)—A person who follows the teachings of Jesus in the New Testament of the Bible.

**civil rights** (SIH-vil RYTS)—Rights that all people should have.

**desegregated** (dee-SEH-greh-gay-ted)—A system that ends the separation of people of different races.

**dignity** (DIG-nih-tee)—Calmness and respect.

**discrimination** (dis-krih-mih-NAY-shun)—Unfair treatment of a group of people.

**equality** (ee-KWH-lih-tee)—Having the same rights as everyone else.

**hate crimes**—Violent acts against someone because of their race or beliefs.

**nonviolent** (non-VY-lent)—Without physical fighting.

**protest** (PROH-test)—To act to change something you believe is unfair.

**reverend** (REH-vrend)—A preacher.

**sanitation** (saa-nih-TAY-shun)—The process of cleaning, such as by removing garbage.

**segregation** (seh-greh-GAY-shun)— Separating people because of their race.

**sit-ins**—Protests held by sitting in racially segregated businesses where people of the sitters' race are not wanted.

**society** (suh-SY-uh-tee)—A group of people.

**unjust** (un-JUST)—Legally unfair.

# INDEX

Abernathy, Ralph  20, 21, 25
Atlanta, Georgia  9, 13, 26
civil rights  5, 19, 23, 27
desegregated buses  21
Dexter Avenue Baptist Church  12, 14, 15
discrimination  5, 9, 11
Ebenezer Baptist Church  8, 13
Gandhi, Mohandas K.  23, 24
hate crimes  19
India  23, 24
Jackson, Jesse  25, 26
Jim Crow laws  11
Johnson, Lyndon B.  24
Kennedy, John F.  24
King, Alberta Williams (mother)  9–10, 13
King, Alfred Daniel (brother)  9, 13
King, Christine (sister)  9
King, Coretta Scott (wife)  14–15, 24, 26, 27
King, Martin Luther Jr.
  arrest of  20
  birth of  9
  birthday of  26–27
  children of  14–15
  death of  25–26
  education of  12, 13
  marriage of  14
  as preacher  12, 13, 15
  speeches of  5–7, 25
King, Martin Luther Sr. (father)  9–11, 12, 13, 14
Lincoln Memorial  5
Lorraine Hotel  25
March on Washington  5–7
Martin Luther King Jr. Day  27
Martin Luther King Jr. Memorial Center  26
Montgomery, Alabama  12, 15, 17–18, 21, 23–24
Montgomery Bus Boycott  16, 17–19, 20, 24
Montgomery Improvement Association  17–18
Morehouse College  13
National Association for the Advancement of Colored People (NAACP)  18
New England Conservatory of Music  14
Nixon, E.D.  17, 18
Nobel Peace Prize  22, 23
nonviolence  19, 23, 24
Parks, Rosa  16, 17, 18
Randolph, A. Philip  4
Reagan, Ronald  27
Rustin, Bayard  4, 20
segregation  6, 9, 11, 16, 19, 21
sit-ins  24
Smiley, Glenn  21
Southern Christian Leadership Conference (SCLC)  5, 25
United States Supreme Court  6, 19
Washington, D.C.  4, 5–7, 26
Williams, Adam Daniel (grandfather)  8
Williams, Hosea (aide)  25
Williams, Jennie Celeste (grandmother)  8